123
SESAME STREET®

Grover's Magic Carpet Ride

By Michaela Muntean
Adapted by Susan Rich Brooke
Illustrated by Tom Brannnon
Grover performed by Eric Jacobson

publications international, ltd.

Play-a-Story™ Animated Storybook

Here are my dresser and toys. Here is my bed. And here is my cute, fuzzy little rug.

Oh, so fuzzy!

Sometimes I, Grover, like to pretend that my rug is not an ordinary rug. I pretend it is a magic carpet.

Whenever I want to go somewhere, all I have to do is sit on my carpet. I close my eyes and think hard about where I would like to go.

Then I open my eyes, and I am on my way. I am flying through the air on my magic carpet!

Ooooh, the clouds look like different shapes, just like they do from the ground. But they are much, MUCH bigger way up here.

That cloud looks like a great big plate of yummy mashed potatoes.

Mmmm m!

And this one looks like a

very large

vet cuddly bunny.

Oh, and here is a very handsome cloud.

And that one must be Cloud Nine!

I wonder where I should go next on my magic carpet ride. Hmmm, I can go anywhere in the whole wide world. I know! I will go visit my grandma. She will be so surprised to see me!

My, it did not take long at all to get to Grandma's house.

Hello, Grandma!

Oh dear, I did not know it was so tricky to park a magic carpet.

Next time, I must be more careful where I land. It is not easy for a small monster like myself to get down from such a tall roof.

You know, there is always room for two on a magic carpet.

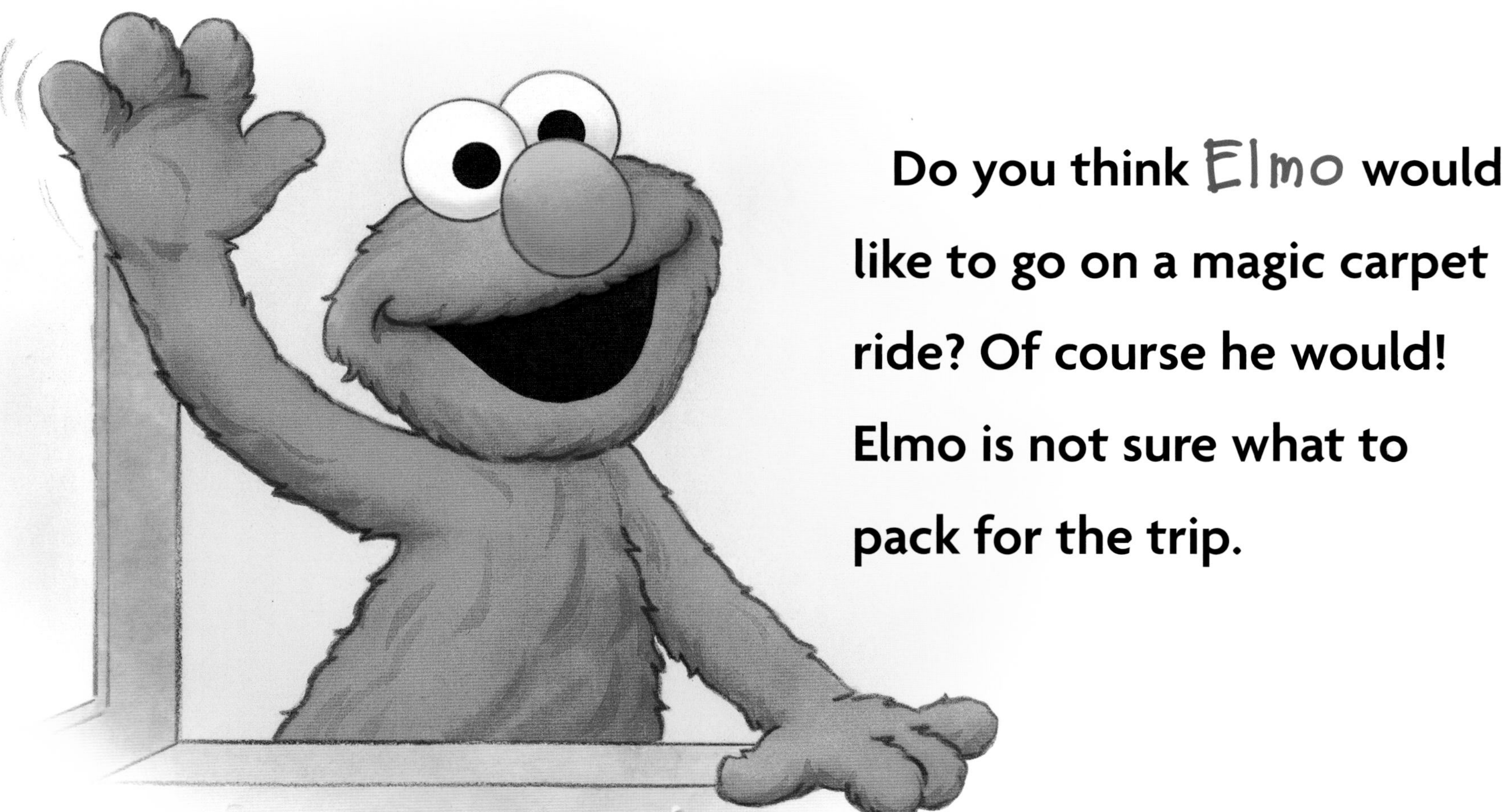

Do you think Elmo would like to go on a magic carpet ride? Of course he would! Elmo is not sure what to pack for the trip.

We decide that he cannot go wrong with some peanut butter and jelly sandwiches.

Hop on, Elmo. Time to take off! Up, up, and away!

Elmo would like to go to the seashore. When we both imagine, we can get there twice as fast.

Maybe... TOO fast?

Here comes the seashore!

There goes the seashore! Oh, and here is the sea!

I really must be more careful about those landings. Now my fuzzy little magic carpet is a soggy little magic carpet.

While the magic carpet dries in the sun, Elmo and I **go swimming...**

and collect seashells...

and build a sandcastle.

Elmo likes building sandcastles a little bit more than I do.

The next place we decide to visit is Paris, France. Paris is a long, long way away, so there is enough time for us to eat lunch on the flight.

Do you see that up ahead? It is the Eiffel Tower.

Ooh la la!

The Eiffel Tower is quite an eye-full. Ha! There is no place to land a magic carpet. Oh well, we will just fly around and around... and around... and around... and around. Whoa! Oh, some little French birdies have come along for the ride.

The Eiffel Tower is very high... but it is not high enough for us! We want to fly somewhere even higher, like a snowcapped mountain.

Wheeee! Look, Elmo! No hands!

Snow is very slippery, so I will imagine the magic carpet is a magic sled.

Whew! Now we are right at the tippy-top of the **tallest** mountain. It is also the coldest mountain. No problem! My wonderful magic carpet will keep us toasty warm.

Brrr

Hmmm.
There is nothing to see but snow at the top of this mountain—until I, Grover, imagine some **mountain goats.**

Just for fun, Elmo and I decide to go to a baseball game. First we fly high above the countryside. Oh my! The cows and horses and sheep look like teeny-tiny little toys. Look at them!

Now we are flying clear across the city. The people on the ground are looking up and wondering what is flying by.

No, it is I, Grover!

We reach the baseball game just as the batter hits the ball. It lands right in Elmo's hand! Now that is what I call a fly ball!

It is getting late. Elmo and I need to get back home. But we are not ready to stop imagining just yet.

I, Grover, have an idea! We can go back home the long way around.

So we fly back over the baseball game,

back over the mountains,

back over Paris,

and back over the seashore...

all the way back to Elmo's house!

Then I swoop down to the ground on my magic carpet and drop Elmo off at his front door. Bye-bye, Elmo!

Traveling is fun, but it is always nice to be home again...
especially when a little monster is feeling sleepy.